Let's Go

Beach!

By Lori Haskins Houran

Illustrated by Nila Aye

A GOLDEN BOOK · NEW YORK

Text copyright © 2021 by Lori Haskins Houran
Cover art and interior illustrations copyright © 2021 by Nila Aye
All rights reserved. Published in the United States by Golden Books, an imprint of
Random House Children's Books, a division of Penguin Random House LLC, 1745 Broadway,
New York, NY 10019. Golden Books, A Golden Book, A Little Golden Book, the G colophon, and
the distinctive gold spine are registered trademarks of Penguin Random House LLC.
rhcbooks.com
Educators and librarians, for a variety of teaching tools, visit us at RHTeachersLibrarians.com
Library of Congress Control Number: 2020934899
ISBN 978-0-593-17462-3 (trade) — ISBN 978-0-593-17463-0 (ebook)
Printed in the United States of America
10 9 8 7 6 5 4 3 2 1

It was hot. Too hot.
"I'm melting," I moaned.
"Me too," said Mom.

"There's only one place to be on a day like this," Dad said. "Let's go to the beach!"
"WOO-HOO!" I cried.

Mom and I raced to put on our swimsuits.
I put mine on a little too fast.

The beach was packed.

"Here's a good spot," I said.
We set up our umbrella. It felt like Mom
put a whole bottle of sunscreen on me.

Finally, it was time to swim!

"The water's nice," I called. "Come in, Dad."

SPLASH!

Dad jumped in and gasped. "Oh! It's FREEZING!"

He falls for it every time.

I saw some friends from my street.

We jumped in the waves.

We searched for seashells.

We made sand angels.
I got a tiny bit sandy.

"Lu-unch!" called Mom.

Sandwiches always taste better at the beach.
Even when they're crunchy.

"Hey!" I cried.
A seagull stole my sandwich!

Good thing Mom had packed an extra one.

After lunch, Dad read me a story
under the umbrella.

"One more swim?" asked Mom.

We swam and swam. When our arms wore out, we floated on our backs.

TWEET! The lifeguard blew his whistle. "Beach closes in ten minutes," he called.

"Thanks," Mom told him. "What a day!"
"It was a hot one," he said. "It's going to be
even hotter tomorrow."

Mom looked at me.
"There's only one place to be on a day like that,"
she said. "Let's come back to the beach!"

"WOO-HOO!"